For Arthur Ed
with love from Mummy – M. R.

For Lou, Finn & Tilly - all my love x – N. E.

★

PUFFIN BOOKS
Published by the Penguin Group: London, New York,
Australia, Canada, India, Ireland, New Zealand and South Africa
Penguin Books Ltd, Registered Offices: 80 Strand, London WC2R 0RL, England
puffinbooks.com
First published 2012
007
Text copyright © Michelle Robinson, 2012
Illustrations copyright © Nick East, 2012
All rights reserved
The moral right of the author and illustrator has been asserted
Made and printed in China
ISBN: 978–0–141–34284–9

Goodnight Digger

PUFFIN

Michelle Robinson

Illustrated by **Nick East**

It's time for bed.
Turn down the light.
Let's tidy up and
say goodnight.

Goodnight fire truck.

Goodnight plane.

Goodnight
tipper.

Goodnight train.

Goodnight bus,
  and even bigger,
    best of all, say . . .

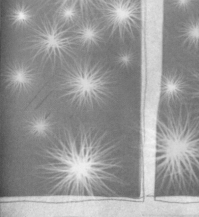

Goodnight digger.

Goodnight chopper.

Goodnight van.

Goodnight tractor.
Goodnight tram.

Goodnight boat,
and even bigger,
best of all, say . . .

Goodnight digger.

Goodnight
lorries.

Goodnight rockets.

Goodnight cars
and trucks in pockets.

Fire truck, chopper, van and plane.

Tipper, tractor, tram and train.

Lorries,

rockets,

trucks

and cars.

Bus and boat

and moon and stars.

Goodnight all, and even bigger,

best of all, say . . .

Goodnight digger.